Peppa's Happy Halloween!

A GOLDEN BOOK · NEW YORK

This book is based on the TV series Peppa Pig. Peppa Pig is created by Neville Astley and Mark Baker.
Peppa Pig © Astley Baker Davies Ltd/Entertainment One UK Ltd 2003.

www.peppapig.com

ISBN 978-0-593-11846-7
rhcbooks.com
Printed in the United States of America
10 9 8 7 6 5 4 3 2 1
2019 Golden Books Edition

Peppa loves to dress up for Halloween.
Use the key to color this picture.

KEY

1 = light pink
2 = magenta
3 = purple
4 = brown

Help Peppa get to Mr. Zebra so she can send out her Halloween party invitations.

START

FINISH

Answers on page 47

3

Peppa is dressed like a witch.
Which witch is different from the rest?

Find a sticker of the different
witch and place it here.

4

Answers on page 47

Mummy and Daddy Pig carve a jack-o-lantern for Halloween.
Can you find the three differences in the second picture?

Answers on page 47

Draw a line from each tiger to who they really are underneath the face paint.

Answers on page 47

George is dressed as his favorite toy.
Use the code below to find out what he is.

A	D	O	N	R	S	I	U
1	2	3	4	5	6	7	8

0 1 2 3 4 5 6 7 8 9 10

__ __ __ __ __ __ __ __ __
1 2 7 4 3 6 1 8 5

Answers on page 47

Answers on page 47

Decorate these yummy cupcakes
for Peppa's Halloween party.

Peppa dresses like a magician for Halloween.
Draw something that Peppa has made appear
with her special wand.

Suzy Sheep is dressed like an astronaut for Halloween.
Which path will get her to the toy rocket ship?

Answers on page 47

Get Peppa to Suzy Sheep
so they can go trick-or-treating.

START

FINISH

Answers on page 47

Candy Cat loves Halloween!
Draw her a trick-or-treat bag full of candy.

Make Halloween cards for your friends and family!

- Have a grown-up help you cut out the cards in this book.

- Fill out the cards. Then decorate them with your stickers.

- Give your cards to friends and family.

SPOOKY & sweet

BOO!

Happy
Halloween!

To

_____

From

_____

Happy
Halloween!

To
_____

From
_____

One of these spiders is not like the others.
Find it and circle it.

Answers on page 47

Halloween is a time for tasty treats!
Find and circle some Halloween treats below.

How many did you find? Write the number here.

_____

Now add treat stickers to make the total number 10.

Answers on page 47

Peppa and George enjoy their trick-or-treat goodies.
Draw your favorite Halloween treat.

Match these partying pirates to their names.

Peppa

Suzy

Zoe

Answers on page 47

Draw a line from each of Peppa's friends
to the name of their costume.

Dinosaur   Pirate   Clown   Carrot

Answers on page 48

HAPPY HALLOWEEN

SPOOKY

BOO!

sweet

TRICK OR TREAT

Connect the dots to see who is dancing at the Halloween party.

Answers on page 48

Help Little Red Riding Peppa get to the Halloween party at the school.

FINISH

START

Answers on page 48

This is a Halloween tree—it grows candy!
Add candy stickers to the tree.

Design the perfect
trick-or-treat bag for Peppa.

Grandpa Pig is having the partygoers look for bags of chocolate coins in the garden.

Circle each bag you find. Write the number here.

_____

George loves to dress up as a robot. Find and circle the picture of Robot George that is different from the rest.

Answers on page 48

31

George is pretending to be a brave explorer for Halloween. Draw something he would be happy to discover.

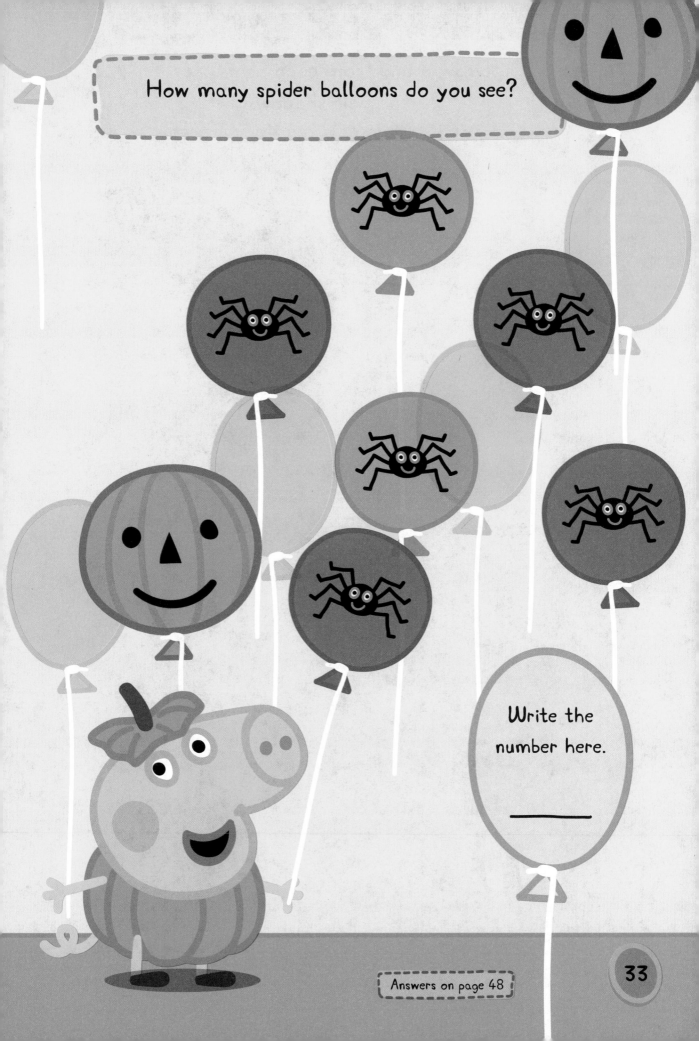

How many spider balloons do you see?

Write the
number here.

_____

Draw a line from each character
to their shadow.

Answers on page 48

Look closely at those ears to figure out who is underneath the costume. Then give him a sticker for best costume.

Fill in each of the blank spaces with the
letter B to see what Peppa is for Halloween.

__usy __uzzing __ee

Answers on page 48

Granny Pig baked a pumpkin pie for the Halloween party.
Make the party festive by adding Halloween balloon stickers.

Halloween Treats!
(A game for two players)

Take turns with a friend connecting two dots with a straight line. When the line you draw completes a square, put your initials in the square and give yourself two points. If the square has candy in it, give yourself two extra points. When all the boxes have been made, whoever has more points wins!

Play again!

It isn't Halloween without bats and black cats!
How many of each can you find and circle?

Now add stickers to make five of each.

I found ____ bats.

I found ____ cats.

40

Answers on page 48

What a fun Halloween party! Can you find three
things that are different in the second picture below?

Answers on page 48

Circle the Halloween costume
that you like the best.

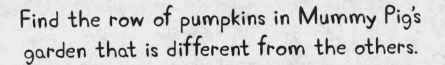

Find the row of pumpkins in Mummy Pig's garden that is different from the others.

1.

2.

3.

4.

5.

Answers on page 48

George is dressed as an astronaut.
Use your stickers to decorate the sky.

Rebecca looks so pretty in her ballerina costume.
Use the key to color this picture.

KEY

1 = yellow
2 = pink
3 = light blue

Happy Halloween!

Answers

Page 3

Page 4

Page 5

Page 11
Path A

Page 6

Page 7

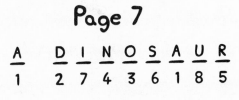

A / 1   D / 2   I / 7   N / 4   O / 3   S / 6   A / 1   U / 8   R / 5

Page 12

Page 8

Page 19

Page 20
6

Page 23

Peppa

Suzy

Zoe

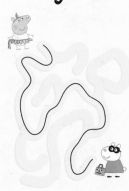

47

Answers

Page 24

Dinosaur   Pirate   Clown   Carrot

Page 25

Page 26

Page 29
7

Page 30

Page 33
6

Page 34

Page 35
Edmond Elephant

Page 36
Busy **B**uzzing **B**ee

Page 40
I found __4__ bats.

I found __3__ cats.

Page 41

Page 43
Row 4